I'm Walking, I'm Running, I'm Jumping, I'm Hopping . . .

Richard Harris

Illustrated by R. Craig Harris

HAMPTON ROADS
PUBLISHING COMPANY, INC.

for the evolving human spirit

Cover design by Marjoram Productions
Cover art by R. Craig Harris

RTH ENT
One Columbus Center, Suite 800
283 Constitution Drive
Virginia Beach, VA 23462-6782
Or call: 757-493-8265
FAX: 757-493-8266
e-mail: rtharris@LNC.com

Distributed by:
Hampton Roads Publishing Company
1125 Stoney Ridge Road
Charlottesville, VA 22902

Or call: 434-296-2772
FAX: 434-296-5096
e-mail: hrpc@hrpub.com
www.hrpub.com

If you are unable to order this book from your local bookseller, you may order directly from the publisher.
757-493-8265
FAX: 757-493-8266

Library of Congress Catalog Card Number: 2005903854

ISBN: 0-9704504-1-9
10 9 8 7 6 5 4 3 2 1

Printed on acid-free paper in China

Dedicated to my two grandchildren, Caroline and Katie,
who keep me "Walking and Running and Jumping and Hopping."

A special thanks to Fran Johnson, Mary Beth Kelly,
Mary Beth Lemanski, Missy Lipkin, Donna McCoy,
Bill Pascarosa, Dr. David Swain, and Wareings' Gym,
who all made a significant contribution.

To my wife, Carol, and my children, Kelly, Corey, and Craig,
I say "Thank You!" for their loving encouragement.

I'm walking, I'm running, I'm jumping, I'm hopping.

My body's in motion with no sign of stopping.

I'm skipping, I'm climbing, I'm catching, I'm throwing,

I'm biking, I'm hiking, I'm coming and going.

All of these actions are good for your heart,

And I'm into living, so I'm doing my part.

I can walk by myself, I can walk with others.

I can walk with my parents, my sisters and brothers.

Sometimes I walk slow, sometimes I walk fast.

The point is I'm walking so my body will last.

All of these activities are good for your lungs

And I'm into living to keep myself young.

I sit up, I push up, I pull up to get stronger.

I swim and ride bikes till I can't go any longer.

I'm bouncing, I'm hanging, I'm twisting, I'm turning.

I'm swinging, I'm singing, the calories are burning.

All this activity is good for your muscles

And I'm into living so I'm willing to hustle.

I'm better at some things than I am at others.

But so are my friends and my sisters and brothers.

I can run fast but my brother jumps higher.

My sister jumps rope like her feet are on fire.

I'm reading, I'm learning, my brain wheels are turning.

I learn about fitness and keep my legs churning.

If you're hurt or sick, go see your physician;

Let the "Doc" check you out, then make your decision.

The decision to be active should not be "yes" or "no."

But whether to start fast or take it real slow.

No matter your age be you younger or older

Keep your body in motion, to be stronger and bolder!

One part of staying healthy is proper nutrition:

Eating GOOD FOOD builds your physical condition.

I eat fresh fruits, apples and oranges and grapes;

They come in all colors and sizes and shapes.

Vegetables too are so good for your health

And help you grow strong and gain body wealth.

The smarter you eat, the better you'll feel,

And when you're ill, good food helps your body heal.

Carbohydrates (or sugars), fats and protein

Are building blocks and fuel for the human machine.

Protein and carbs and unsaturated fat:

A whole lot of this, some of them, less of that.

One way to stay healthy is watch what you eat:

Vegetables and fruits and grain foods and meat,

Nuts and cherries and cereal with strawberries,

Oatmeal and whole wheat with milk from the dairies,

Tomatoes and carrots and spinach and such

Provide vitamins and minerals our bodies need so much.

The body is efficient, a wonderful machine

That wants to work smoothly, look fit and stay lean.

The food you don't use, your body will store.

So if you're not moving, it stores more and more!

Controlling your weight is a rather simple matter.

Exercise and reduce the size of your platter.

I bend and I stretch to loosen my limbs;

I warm up and work out and try to stay trim.

When my body is fine-tuned, then I'm at my best

Through proper nutrition, exercise, and rest!

When your body is fit, I'm sure you'll find

You`ll feel smarter; it refreshes your mind.

Train with resistance (weights) when you want to get stronger.

Aerobic training (consistence) helps to stay stronger, longer!

Twisting and stretching helps improve your reach.

Lifting and aerobics gets you fit for the beach!

All of the activities are good for your heart,

And I'm into living and I want to live smart.

One day you may find you're the "Crème de la Crème"

And want to be a part of an athletic team.

You'll learn a new skill, then practice and drill.

Improve your performance? You certainly will!

Whether you compete or you do it for fun,

Exercise and eat well to stay fit for the long run!

Exercise the body to keep the blood flowing;

Feed it and rest it, keep it thriving and growing.

Age is no reason nor offers excuse,

For neglecting your body or for physical misuse.

Regardless of age or of size or background,

Now is the time to begin to crack down.

A key to good health is to get a good education,

Then practice what you learn with zeal and moderation!

Set your goal, get on a roll, keep track of how you're doing.

Get in a groove, keep on the move, you'll save your body from ruin.

Make up your mind and you will find there's really nothing to it;

Make it fun when you walk or run but the main thing is,

JUST DO IT!